D0262284

Stories of Snowmen

Russell Punter

Illustrated by Philip Webb

Reading Consultant: Alison Kelly
Roehampton University

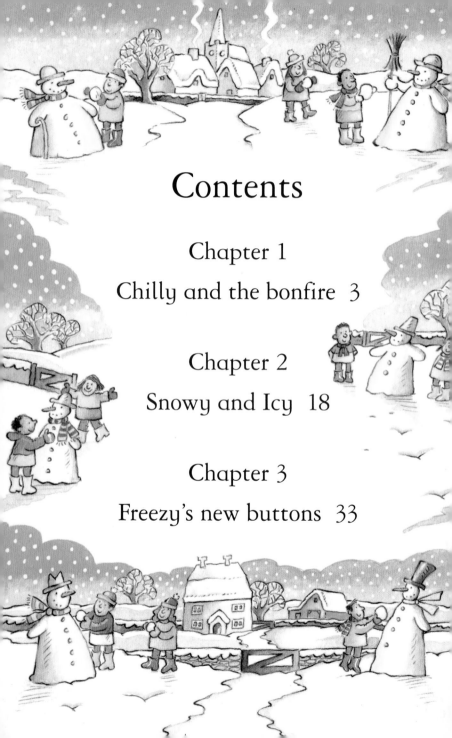

Contents

Chapter 1

Chilly and the bonfire 3

Chapter 2

Snowy and Icy 18

Chapter 3

Freezy's new buttons 33

Chapter 1

Chilly and the bonfire

Jack pulled back his bedroom curtains. A fresh blanket of snow covered the ground.

Pulling on warm clothes, he ran out into the crunchy snow. "I'm going to build the best snowman ever," Jack thought.

First he made the body...

then he rolled a snowball for the head...

added two black
pebbles for eyes...

four more for a
smiley mouth...

stuck in a carrot
for a nose...

and finished
off with a hat
and scarf.

Jack stood back to admire his new snowman.

"I'll call you Chilly," he said proudly.

Jack heard banging from the field next door. Mr. Oats was putting up a sign.

Grand Christmas Party

Oats' Farm - Saturday Dec 24th 6:00pm

Music, Dancing, Games,
Hot Chocolate, Toasted Marshmallows,
Blazing Bonfire
Buy your tickets at the farm shop

Jack licked his lips. He loved
toasted marshmallows.

"Can I come to your party,
please?" he asked the farmer.

"Of course, Jack," replied Mr. Oats. "I'll let you in for free if you help me build the bonfire."

Jack climbed over the fence and picked up an armful of logs. In no time, he and Mr. Oats had built a huge bonfire.

But, the next morning, it had vanished.

New footprints led from Jack's house to where the bonfire had been.

"What have you done with my bonfire?" shouted Mr. Oats.

"It wasn't me," sniffed Jack.

"I don't like people playing tricks on me," said the farmer. "You're banned from the party."

Jack felt terrible.
Mr. Oats built a new bonfire and stomped home.

That night, Jack couldn't get
to sleep. "Who would steal a
bonfire?" he asked himself.

Just then, he heard the
clattering of wood outside.
Jack raced out of the house.

Jack couldn't believe his eyes. Chilly the snowman was taking down the bonfire.

W...what's going on?

"Oh no," cried the snowman nervously. "We're not supposed to let people see us move."

12

"You're alive!" gasped Jack.
"Of course," said Chilly. "All snowmen come alive at night."

"So *you* took the bonfire?" said Jack.
"Yes," said Chilly, looking ashamed.
"But why?" asked Jack.

13

"It was so close, I would have melted," explained Chilly. "I didn't want that to happen. You made me so well."

"Why didn't you just run away?" asked Jack.

Chilly shook his head. "A snowman must return to where he was built," he said firmly.

"I didn't mean to get you into trouble," added Chilly sadly.

"Don't worry," said Jack. "All we have to do is move the fire."

Jack and his icy new friend carried the logs to the middle of the field.

The pair spent all night
building the new bonfire.
Chilly returned to his place
just before Mr. Oats arrived.

"I've built you an even better
bonfire, Mr. Oats," said Jack.
"To make up for the one you
lost. I think it looks much
better over here."

Mr. Oats was so impressed,
he let Jack go to the party.

And only Jack noticed the
snowman next door give him
a grateful wink.

Chapter 2

Snowy and Icy

The children of Frostly were hard at work. Tomorrow was judging day of the Best Snowman Contest.

18

Emma Humble was finishing her snowman, Snowy.

He had a battered felt hat...

tiny stones for his eyes and mouth...

a moth-eaten woolly scarf...

and a broken old walking stick.

Daphne Dosh lived next
door. She was so rich, she had
servants to build her snowman,
Icy. He had a shiny top hat...

sparkly buttons
for his eyes
and mouth...

a spotted
silk scarf...

and a silver-
topped cane.

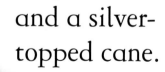

Daphne peered over the fence at Emma.

"Icy is twice as nice as your snowman," she boasted.

"At least I built Snowy myself," said Emma.

"Ha," scoffed Daphne. "We'll see who's best tomorrow."

That night, the snowmen of Frostly came to life.

Icy pointed at Snowy. "What a frightful sight," he jeered.

Snowy looked at his tattered clothes with his stony eyes.

"You'll never win the contest," said Icy smugly.

"Maybe I can make myself look better," said Snowy. He set off across the fields.

Icy was certain he'd be the best snowman in town. But he decided to follow Snowy just to make sure.

Snowy saw some sheep's wool caught on a wire fence. "I could use that to patch up my scarf," he thought.

Icy crept up behind Snowy. "We'll see how your scarf looks after it's been tangled in that wire," he chortled to himself.

24

Icy was about to push Snowy into the fence when he heard a loud 'Baaaa!'

A flock of sheep raced by and knocked him down.

Snowy took the wool and entered the woods. "That twisty branch would make a great walking stick," he said.

Icy climbed a tree behind Snowy. "I'll get you this time, stony face," thought Icy.

Icy began sawing through a heavy branch. "This will put a dent in Snowy's hat," he chuckled.

But the silly snowman had cut through the branch he was sitting on...

Icy fell out of the tree
and landed in a prickly
holly bush.

Snowy tucked his new
stick under his arm and
walked on.

Snowy came to an icy pond.
Lots of shiny round pebbles
lay around the edge.

"These will make great buttons," thought Snowy.
Icy tip-toed up behind him.

Icy went to push Snowy into the pond. But as he did so, Snowy bent over to pick up a handful of pebbles.

29

Icy flew over Snowy, slid silently across the ice and vanished into a patch of reeds.

Snowy put on his new buttons and plodded back to Emma's house.

He admired his new stick and buttons, then he mended his scarf. He didn't notice Icy stagger home much later.

The sneaky snowman was a lumpy mess and he was covered in leaves and reeds.

The next day, the snowmen
were judged. Scruffy Icy came
last and Snowy won first prize.
Daphne was furious.

Emma was thrilled. But
she never found out how her
snowman got his new outfit.

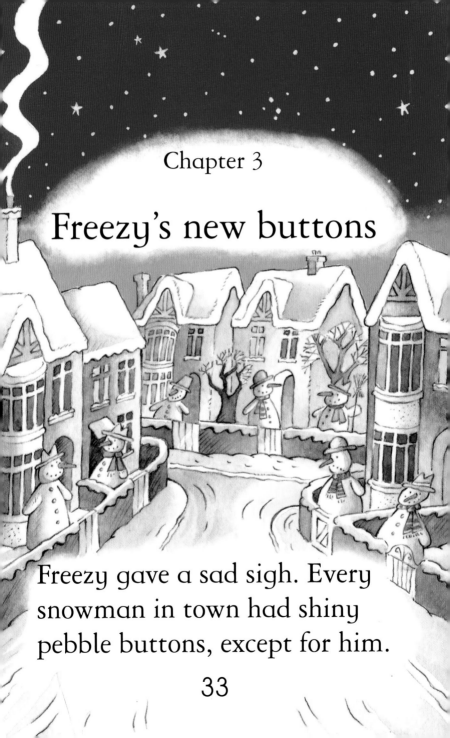

Chapter 3

Freezy's new buttons

Freezy gave a sad sigh. Every snowman in town had shiny pebble buttons, except for him.

Crispy had three big buttons...

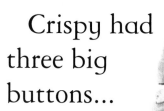

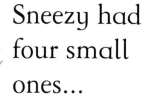

Sneezy had four small ones...

and Shiver had eight of all shapes and sizes.

That afternoon, two men rushed along Freezy's street. "Where can we hide 'em, Stan?" panted one.

"I've got an idea, Lenny," gasped the other. He pulled a little bag from his pocket.

Stan took three shiny stones
from the bag and stuck them
in Freezy's chest.

"Buttons!" laughed Lenny.

"Let's get out of here," said
Stan. The sneaky pair ran off
as quickly as they had arrived.

Freezy was dying to show off his new buttons. But he had to wait until night time.

As soon as it got dark, Freezy visited his friends. "What do you think of my buttons?" he said with a grin.

"Wow! They're so sparkly," gasped Crispy.

"Better than pebbles!" cried Sneezy.

"Where did you get them?" asked Shiver.

38

"Oh, they were a present," said Freezy proudly.

His friends were so jealous, their snow nearly turned green.

Freezy strolled home. As he walked along, a newspaper blew around his feet.

The newspaper headline
nearly melted him with shock.

The EVENING BLAB

JEWEL THIEVES STEAL DIGBY DIAMONDS

Stan Snatch

Crooks get away
with three jewels
worth 1 million
from Christmas
display

The diamonds

Lenny Grab

Freezy was wearing stolen
jewels. "I'd better hand them
in to the police," he thought.

At that moment, he heard a
familiar voice behind him.
"There he is, Lenny!"
The two crooks raced up.

To the thieves' amazement,
Freezy ran off in fright.
"He's *alive?*" screamed Lenny.
"After him!" yelled Stan.

The crooks chased Freezy up into the hills.

Freezy stopped to catch his breath. He was exhausted. "They're bound to catch me soon," he puffed.

Then he had an idea.

When the crooks caught up with Freezy, they found him sitting under a ledge.

"He's taken the jewels off his chest," said Lenny.

"Hand 'em over, snow features!" barked Stan.

43

"I'm sorry," said Freezy. "I can't hear you."

"Where are the diamonds?" yelled Lenny.

"Excuse me?" said Freezy.

"Where are the jewels?" roared Stan.

"Speak up," said Freezy.

The crooks' shouting made the snow on the hillside shake. With a huge whoosh, it thundered down.

Freezy took the diamonds from under his hat and stuck them in the snow.

He pulled Stan's phone from his pocket and called the police. He told them where to find the crooks and the jewels.

Then Freezy ran off so the
police wouldn't see him.
But perhaps they did...

The next day, a policeman
pinned a shiny gold medal to
Freezy's scarf. That was even
better than a button.

Series editor:
Lesley Sims

First published in 2007 by Usborne Publishing Ltd., Usborne House,
83-85 Saffron Hill, London EC1N 8RT, England. www.usborne.com
Copyright © 2007 Usborne Publishing Ltd.